GUTENBERG

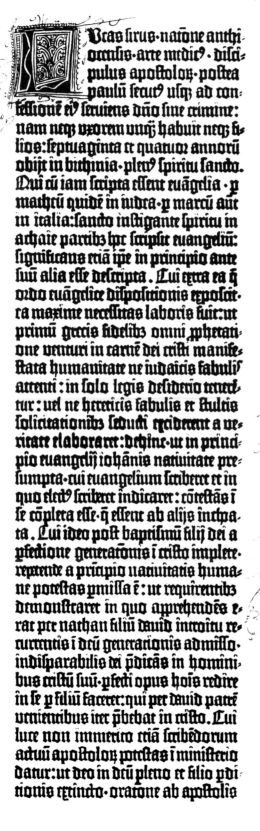

Vcas sirus·natōne anthi
occnsis·arte medic⁹·disci
pulus apostoloꝝ·postea
paulū secut⁹ vsꝗ ad con
fessionē eī seruiens dūo siue crimine·
nam neꝗ vxorem vnꝗ habuit neꝗ fi
lios:septuaginta et quatuor annorū
obijt in bithinia·plen⁹ spiritu sancto.
Qui cū iam scripta essent euāgelia·ꝑ
mathcū quidē in iudea·ꝑ marcū aūt
in italia:sancto instigante spiritu in
achaie partibꝫ hꝛc scripsit euangeliū:
significans etiā iꝑe in principio ante
suū alia esse descripta·Cui extra ea ꝗ
ordo euāgelice dispositionis exposcit
ra maxime necessitas laboris fuit:ut
primū grecis fidelibꝫ omni ꝓphetati
one venturi in carne dei cristi manife
stata humanitate ne iudaicis fabulis
attenti:in solo legis desiderio tenerē
tur:vel ne hereticis fabulis et stultis
solicitationibꝫ seducti excidcrent a ve
ritate elaboraret:bethinc·ut in princi
pio euangelij iohānis natiuitate pre
sumpta·cui euangelium scriberet et in
quo elect⁹ scriberet indicaret:cōtestās ī
se cōpleta esse·ꝗ essent ab alijs inchoa
ta·Cui ideo post baptismū filij dei a
ꝑfectione generatōnis ī cristo implere
reptende a principio natiuitatis huma
ne potestas ꝑmissa ē:ut requirentibꝫ
demonstraret in quo apprehendēs e
rat ꝑ nathan filiū dauid introitu re
currentis ī dcū generationis admisso·
indisparabilis dei ꝑdicās in homini
bus cristū suū·ꝑfecti opus hois redire
in se ꝑ filiū faceret:qui per dauid patrē
venientibus iter ꝑbebat in cristo. Cui
luce non immerito etiā scribēdorum
actuū apostoloꝝ potestas ī ministerio
datur:ut deo in dcū pleno et filio ꝑdi
tionis extincto·oratione ab apostolis

facta·sorte domini electionis numer⁹
compleretur:sicꝫ paulus cōsumma
tione apostolicis actibꝫ daret·quē dīu
cōtra stimulū recalcitrantē dūs elegis
set. Quod et legentibꝫ ac requirentibꝫ
dcū·et si per singula expediri a nobis
vtile fuerat:sciens tame ꝗ operātem
agricolā oportcat de suis fructibus e
dere·vitauim⁹ publicā curiositatem:
ne nō tā volentibꝫ dcū demōstrare vide
rentur·quā fastidientibus prodidisse.

Alius prologus

Voniā quidē multi co
nati sūt ordinare nar
ratiōnes ꝗ ī nobis com
plete sūt reꝛ·sicut tradi
derūt nobis ꝗ ab initio
iꝑi viderūt·et ministri
fuerūt sermonis:visū ē et michi assecuto
oīa a principio diligēter ex ordie tibi
scribere optīe theophile:ut cognoscas
eoꝛ verboꝛ de ꝗbꝫ eruditꝰ es veritatē. ca͞p· l̄

Vit in diebus herodis re
gis iudee sacerdos quidam
nomine zacharias de vi
ce abia·et vxor illi de filia
bus aaron:et nomen eius elizabeth.
Erant autem iusti ambo ante deum:
incedentes in omnibus mandatis z
iustificationibus domini sine quere
la·Et non erat illis filius·eo ꝗ es
set elizabeth sterilis:et ambo proces
sissent ī diebus suis. Factū est aūt cū sa
cerdotio fungeretur zacharias in ordi
ne vicis sue ante deū:scdm cōsuetudi
nem sacerdotij sorte exijt ut incensum
poneret ingressus in templū domini.
Et omnis multitudo populi erat orās fo
ris hora incensi. Apparuit autem illi
angelus dūi:stans a dextris altaris

GUTENBERG

LEONARD EVERETT FISHER

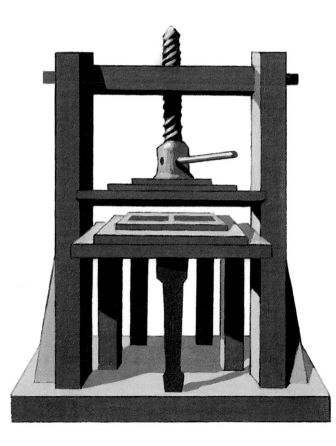

MACMILLAN PUBLISHING COMPANY
New York

Maxwell Macmillan Canada   Toronto

Maxwell Macmillan International   New York   Oxford   Singapore   Sydney

CHRONOLOGY OF JOHANN GUTENBERG

c.1394–1399........Born in Mainz, Germany

1428........Leaves Mainz and settles in Strasbourg

Becomes established in a gemstone cutting and polishing business

1436........Begins experimenting with metal to cast type for printing

1437–1438........Becomes a manufacturer of mirrors and cheap jewelry

Forms a partnership

1442........Is nearly bankrupted

1444-1448........Leaves Strasbourg

Prints copies of *Ars Grammatica*, a grammar book

1448........Borrows money from Arnold Gelthuss

1450........Borrows money from Johann Fust to set up printing business

1452........Borrows more money from Fust and makes him a partner

1454........Begins printing a forty-two-line Bible, assisted by Peter Schoeffer

1456........Loses his business and equipment to Fust, who completes Bible with Schoeffer

1457........Borrows money from Konrad Humery to start new print shop

1457-1460........Prints a thirty-six-line Bible and the *Catholicon*, a dictionary and encyclopedia

Prints an astronomical calendar

1468........Dies in Mainz, Germany

The text of this book is set in 14 pt. Weiss. The black-and-white paintings are rendered in acrylic paints on paper.

With appreciation to Dr. Jacob Smit, Professor of History, Columbia University

Library of Congress Cataloging-in-Publication Data
Fisher, Leonard Everett. Gutenberg / Leonard Everett Fisher. — 1st ed.   p.   cm. Summary: A biography of the fifteenth-century German printer who revolutionized printing with the invention of movable type. ISBN 0-02-735238-2. 1. Gutenberg, Johann, 1397?-1468—Juvenile literature. 2. Printing—History—Origin and antecedents—Juvenile literature. 3. Printers—Germany—Biography—Juvenile literature. [1. Gutenberg, Johann, 1397?-1468. 2. Printers. 3. Printing—History.] I. Title. Z126.Z7F57 1993   686.2'092— dc20   [B]   92-26991

To all the printers, yesterday's, today's, and tomorrow's

Johann Gutenberg is something of a mystery. He was born in Mainz, an ancient town in southwestern Germany that overlooks the Rhine River. The date of his birth is uncertain, but was sometime between 1394 and 1399. No portraits of him were painted in his lifetime. Gutenberg was not even his surname. His parents, Friele and Else Gensfleisch, were Mainz aristocrats. The great house they lived in was called Gutenberg Hof, or "Good Mountain House." Gutenberg might have been called Johann or Hans von Gutenberg—John or Hans of Gutenberg—to distinguish him from relatives who were also named Johann or Hans. And the name stuck.

Although we know little about the man, we are familiar with his achievement: Johann Gutenberg was the creator of modern printing.

During Gutenberg's time, most ordinary people could not read. They had little need of the written word and knew of the world only what they heard or saw. Books were hand-lettered by monks, scribes, and scholars. They were used by churchmen, government leaders, university professors, students, and the educated few—the only people who could read.

By 1428, when Gutenberg was in his twenties, the Hundred Years' War was in its ninety-first year. It was fought off and on between the kings of France and England over which country owned France. Unrest was everywhere in Europe. Petty German princes and corrupt church officials took advantage of this and seized more land and power. When riots against the aristocracy broke out in Mainz, Gutenberg and his family fled to Strasbourg, a city about seventy-five miles to the south.

In Strasbourg, Johann Gutenberg, who knew how to make and use metal punches to create intricate designs in soft gold leaf, began to prosper by cutting and polishing semiprecious stones. There he became obsessed with the idea of printing words mechanically and making many identical copies of them.

In 1436 Gutenberg began to make individual letters out of lead. He cast them into metal strips that were all precisely the same size and thickness.

In 1437 he took Andreas Dritzehn into his business, which now included the making of mirrors and cheap jewelry. A year later Hans Riffe and Andreas Heilmann joined the business. His partners' money gave Gutenberg extra funds with which to secretly continue his work. None of his associates knew what he was up to. Gutenberg aimed to become the only master printer in Europe.

But his partners soon found out. Gutenberg allowed them to invest money in his experiments, and they swore not to reveal them.

Andreas Dritzehn died on December 25, 1439. His relatives, who knew nothing of Gutenberg's printing projects, claimed his place in the business. Gutenberg refused to accept them. They took him to court and lost.

Riffe and Heilmann disappeared soon afterward. Gutenberg's business faded away, and he lived on small rents from family property in Mainz. He continued to experiment alone with metal typecasting and the construction of printing presses modeled after wine and linen presses. But by 1442 he had exhausted his cash and was nearly bankrupt.

Other printers in Europe also may have been experimenting with printing processes. But Gutenberg was the only printer known to be using movable metal type. Gutenberg's method was no longer a secret.

Gutenberg slowly continued to perfect his process of creating metal type by pouring molten lead into precision molds that he had made. He managed to sell whatever he printed. But the upkeep of his press and the expense of materials like paper, inks, oils, cleaning solvents, lead and other metals was proving more burdensome than ever.

In 1450 Gutenberg verged on bankruptcy once again. Then a wealthy Mainz lawyer, Johann Fust, saw the business possibilities in Gutenberg's press. He envisioned a fortune in the printing and selling of unlimited numbers of books. Herr Fust lent Gutenberg a large sum of money to establish a print shop. As security for the loans, Gutenberg used his materials and equipment: type, composing stick (a flat, narrow palette on which letters are arranged into words), chases, type molds, inks and ink balls, paper, oils, cleaning solvents, printing presses, brushes, brooms, and furniture.

Gutenberg ran through the loan in two years and was back where he had started—broke—with little to show for the money. Fust came to the rescue again. But this time the money was not a loan. Johann Fust made himself Gutenberg's partner. Fust expected profits, soon!

Johann Fust turned out to be a scheming partner. In 1456 he took Gutenberg to court, claiming that Gutenberg had never repaid the original loan that had enabled him to set up the print shop. At the time, Gutenberg was still printing copies of the forty-two-line Bible.

The court ordered Gutenberg to repay the loan immediately. Since Gutenberg could not do this, Fust seized all of the materials and equipment in the shop.

Fust then made Peter Schoeffer a full partner. The two of them completed the printing of Gutenberg's Bible. They sold each of the copies for a handsome profit. Gutenberg never saw a florin of the money.

Schoeffer married Fust's daughter. Four generations of Schoeffers continued the printing business that was begun by Gutenberg and so ruthlessly seized by Johann Fust.

Gutenberg, however, was back in business the following year, 1457. Konrad Humery, a wealthy Mainz aristocrat, invested in a new Gutenberg print shop. The deal was the same as before: The money would be secured by all the new materials and equipment. But unlike Johann Fust, Konrad Humery encouraged Gutenberg and presented no threat to his survival.

Gutenberg spent the next three years making new type molds, recasting new type, constructing new presses, and printing a new edition of the Bible with thirty-six lines to a page.

Johann Gutenberg's new printing shop was a busy place. Between 1457 and 1460 he printed the *Catholicon*, a huge Latin dictionary and encyclopedia compiled by Joannes Balbus.

Also, between 1458 and 1459, he managed to print an astronomical calendar. It showed the phases of the moon on given dates, and provided other celestial information for the year, as well.

Until his death on February 3, 1468, Johann Gutenberg went on printing and training young apprentices for the fast-expanding trade of printing.

MORE ABOUT GUTENBERG

Other people, like Laurens Coster of the Netherlands, claimed to have printed with movable type before Gutenberg. Nevertheless, it was Johann Gutenberg's printing process that spread quickly through Europe to change the course of civilization—even through the Far East, where printing had begun. By 1500 there were more than one thousand printers in Europe.

In 1505, thirty-seven years after Gutenberg's death, Johann Schoeffer, the grandson of Johann Fust and son of Peter Schoeffer, acknowledged Gutenberg's contribution in a dedication. It said in part that the book was "printed at Mainz, the town in which the admirable art of typography was invented, in the year 1450, by Johann Gutenberg...."

Gutenberg's movable metal letters and press revolutionized book production, making it possible for millions of people to be reached by the same printed words at nearly the same time. People saw that it was in their best interest to know how to read, to know what was going on in the world. The Age of Information swept over humankind as swiftly as a sharp wind. Johann Gutenberg's vision of the printed word put an end to the Middle Ages and shaped our modern age.